Running
with the Horses

Alison Lester

NorthSouth
New York / London

A LONG TIME AGO, a young girl named Nina lived in a palace that stood in the heart of a graceful old city. The palace was home to the Royal Academy of Dancing Horses, where Nina's father, Viktor, was the stable master.

Every day Viktor and his grooms prepared the white stallions for the academy riders, who guided the horses through their elegant routines. People came from all over the world to see them dancing.

Sometimes Nina's father told her stories about their lives when Nina was little. Back then, they had traveled all over Europe with their own troupe of horses. Nina's mother, Anna, was the star of the show, dancing on their dappled grays like a sequined butterfly.

When Nina was four years old, Anna had died suddenly, leaving Viktor heartbroken. His old friend Karl found him work at the Royal Academy, where Viktor and his little girl could start a new life.

BY THE TIME Nina was ten years old, the academy had closed. A war was raging across the world, and every day the fighting came closer to Nina's city. Theaters and cafés shut down, and the streetlights were dimmed.

One day Nina arrived at her school to find the gates locked and the grounds deserted. She waited in front of the silent buildings, but nobody came. Snowflakes fell from the autumn sky and settled in Nina's hair as she walked home.

The lane beside the palace was usually lined with horse-drawn cabs waiting for passengers. Now it was empty except for Nina's favorite old cab horse, Zelda.

Why have they left you behind? Nina wondered as the old mare nuzzled her pocket for biscuits.

When she arrived home, Nina found her father grooming the stallions.

"My school is closed, Papa," she told him. "And the drivers and cab horses have gone from the lane, except for Zelda."

Victor gathered Nina into his arms. "It's time for us to leave as well," he said. "I have been waiting for the truck to return for these last four horses, but I don't think it's coming now. We will have to take the stallions across the mountains to your grandparents' farm. You will ride with me on my horse."

He placed Nina back on her feet. "Now go and pack. Make sure you bring your warmest clothes."

NINA RAN UPSTAIRS. She felt worried and afraid, but her heart raced with excitement when she thought of riding over the mountains. Until now she had only ever ridden ponies in the park.

After she packed her clothes in her satchel, she picked up the little blue horse her mother had embroidered for her, wrapped it in a woolen shawl, and pushed it deep among her clothes. There was no room for anything else in her bag.

When Viktor came upstairs and made supper that night, Nina had no appetite.

"My darling, you must be brave," Viktor said. "Karl will be with us, and he knows the way."

Nina gave her father a small smile. Karl was her favorite groom at the academy. He always let her help him brush the horses.

Viktor stroked her head. "Now you must go to bed, and I must go to the stables. We leave at dawn."

☾

Nina lay on her bed, but sleep was far away. She kept thinking of Zelda, alone on the street.

Finally she put on her coat and slipped through the passageways of the palace. At an arched doorway, she jiggled the latch open and stepped outside.

ZELDA WHINNIED AS Nina stepped into the lane and ran toward her. Nina put her arms around the old mare and leaned into her neck.

"Oh, Zelda," she murmured, "if everyone is leaving the city, what will happen to you?"

Nina stood on tiptoe, pulled herself up, and wriggled onto the horse's back. Zelda was much taller than the ponies she was used to riding.

Nina closed her eyes and imagined herself and Zelda in the Great Riding Hall. She saw the cheering audience, the glittering chandeliers, and the dazzling spotlights. Nina was riding like her mother, as light as a summer butterfly. She could hear the soaring violins, the cellos, the drums. . . .

NINA SNAPPED OUT of her dream. That sound was not drums at all. It was the crack of gunfire.

"I'm sorry, Zelda," Nina whispered as she slid to the ground. "I have to go."

She raced back through the palace, arriving home seconds before her father burst through the door. Just then a huge explosion shook the building.

"We must leave now!" said Viktor. "We can't wait until morning. Fetch your bag and meet me in the stables."

Nina ran into her room, grabbed her satchel, and hurried out the door. At the foot of the stairs, she paused. She knew her father was waiting in the stables, but she could hear Zelda whinnying outside, so she turned and ran to the lane.

Frantically, Nina untied Zelda, climbed onto her back, and rode into the palace. The night echoed with shouts and gunfire.

When she burst into the bright light of the stables, the stallions reared, wild-eyed.

"Get off that horse!" Viktor ordered. "You are riding with me." He reached for Nina, but she ducked away.

Karl rode between them. "Leave her, Viktor. I know this old horse, and Nina will be all right," he said.

KARL LED THE WAY out of the palace, with Zelda following close behind. Sirens wailed and burning buildings lit the way as the horses raced through the smoky darkness. Nina clung on desperately, but as they skidded around a corner, she cried out, slipping down toward the cobblestones until Viktor reached across and pulled her up.

"Hold onto her mane!" he shouted. "Don't let go!"

Minutes later they reached the park where Nina had once ridden ponies and played with her friends.

"We'll cross here," Karl called out.

Nina looked at the hedge in front of them but couldn't see a gateway. "We have to jump!" her father yelled. He cantered across the grass, and the white horses floated like angels over the hedge. Nina followed, terrified. She closed her eyes, expecting Zelda to crash, but the old horse jumped the hedge easily. They galloped through the park, then raced down the curving boulevard that led out of the city.

NINA CROUCHED LOW as the horses sped along the streets. Suddenly Zelda slammed into the stallions. A huge pile of rubble was blocking the street.

"We're trapped," said Karl. Nina could see the fear on Karl's face.

Just then Zelda turned and trotted toward a narrow alley. Nina tugged on the reins, but the horse ignored her.

"Come back, Nina!" Viktor called, starting to chase after them. The old mare galloped faster, hurtling through the dark streets as if she knew the way. It took all Nina's strength to hold on.

Abruptly they emerged onto a wide road, and Zelda slowed to a walk. The chaos was behind them.

"I'm sorry, Papa," Nina said. "I couldn't stop her."

"No," Viktor replied. "You've done well. This road will take us out of the city."

Karl pointed to the distant mountains, shining blue under the full moon. "That's where we're headed," he said. "We will be safe on the other side."

IT WAS AFTER MIDNIGHT when they reached the foothills of the mountains and finally stopped to rest. Nina turned to look back at the city and gasped. The sky above the buildings was glowing red, as if everything was on fire.

Nina's legs hurt. Without a saddle to sit on, the skin on the inside of her knees had rubbed raw. Viktor bandaged her legs while Karl saddled Zelda, then spread out a blanket and unwrapped some bread and cheese.

After a while they set out again, moving slowly up the trail into the mountains. Nina's saddle felt like an armchair, and she dozed on and off as they rode through the night. She woke as dawn was breaking. It was a cold, clear morning, and the sun shone in stripes through the trees. They kept climbing upward through the forest all morning.

"The trees will hide us," said Viktor as a plane buzzed overhead. "But we won't be safe until we cross the border."

As they rode, Karl told Nina how he had made this journey many times as a young man, taking sheep to summer pasture in the mountains.

"The highest pass marks the border," he said. "That's where I will leave you and return to my family."

Nina was silent, but a shadow of worry settled on her. She had thought Karl would be riding with them all the way.

AT NOON THE RIDERS came to a noisy stream.

"Let's stop here and rest," said Karl.

They unsaddled the horses, and Viktor laid out bread, cheese, and apples on a blanket. After they had eaten, Nina fell asleep while the horses grazed around her. When she awoke, her father was standing with Zelda, hand-feeding her.

"She doesn't want to eat," he said. "It's a bad sign in an old horse, Nina."

Perhaps Zelda was too old for such a hard journey, thought Nina. She bit her lip and led Zelda to the stream, where the horse drank deeply and picked at the water grass. "Come on, girl," Nina whispered. "Please be strong."

When it was time to go, Karl saddled the old mare and helped Nina climb onto Zelda's back.

"We will ride through the night again," he said. "Later, when we cross the ravine, there may be soldiers, but the dark will hide us."

Nina rode behind her father and tried not to think about the soldiers. "How long until we reach the farm, Papa?" she asked.

"We should arrive tomorrow," he said. "It is still a long way."

LATE THAT NIGHT they rode out of the forest. The air felt sharp, and the carpet of pine needles gave way to stones that scraped and rattled under the horses' hooves.

Nina strained her eyes in the dark and could just make out the snow-capped mountains.

"Stay close," Viktor called. "We're nearing the bridge."

The moon was behind the clouds, and the ravine was in darkness. They would be riding blind onto the bridge.

"I'll go first," Viktor said.

His white horses moved forward, but suddenly Zelda pushed past them. Nina screamed as she was almost thrown off. "Zelda! Stop!" she cried as the mare spun around with her ears back and her teeth bared. She struck out with her forelegs, driving the stallions back off the bridge. Nina clung on, terrified.

"Jump off her, Nina!" Karl tried to grab the reins.

Viktor leaped from his horse and pulled her from the saddle. At that moment, the clouds parted and the moon lit the scene before them.

The middle of the bridge had been completely blown away, and a yawning hole gaped above the ravine. Far below, the black river glinted in the moonlight. Nina shivered to think how close they had come to falling in.

They remounted and rode away from the ruined bridge. Under the trees, Karl reined in his horse.

"I know another way," he told them. "It is a longer track, but it will get us to the pass."

As they went on, Nina patted Zelda with a shaky hand.

DAWN BROKE SLOWLY to a heavy gray sky. Nina's hands were so numb with cold, she could hardly hold the reins. Up here in the high mountains the ground was bare and rocky, and the horses picked their way through patches of snow.

"Karl thinks a storm is coming," said Viktor as he handed Nina a piece of bread. "We must cross the pass before it arrives."

As they climbed higher into the clouds, Zelda kept slipping. Nina wanted to get off and walk, but Viktor wouldn't let her.

"You will be exhausted in no time if you walk," he said. "I can see Zelda is tired, but you only feel like a feather on her back."

They rode up through thick mist for another hour, then all at once the horses stepped out into dazzling sunlight. They were above the clouds now, on a snowy plain, with mountain peaks soaring on either side.

Viktor turned to Nina. "This is the pass," he said. "We are crossing the border."

The stallions snorted in the sparkling sunlight, then broke into a trot. They pranced over the plain, sending up flurries of powdery snow. Zelda trailed behind with her head high and her ears pricked forward.

IT WAS TIME for Karl to leave. The sky clouded over as they said good-bye. Karl knelt in the snow and hugged Nina.

"I don't want you to go," she whispered.

"Don't worry," he replied. "We'll ride together again when this war is over. I can see you will be a fine horsewoman."

"She's like her mother," said Viktor. "A natural rider."

Karl waved without looking back as he walked away, and they watched until he disappeared into the mist.

"Come, Nina," Viktor said. "We must keep riding." He ran a hand along the old mare's neck. "I hope she will be all right."

As they began their descent down the other side of the mountain, the snow was almost up to the horses' bellies. Nina's feet felt frozen in her sodden boots, and Zelda's steps were weak and faltering.

SUDDENLY ZELDA STUMBLED and fell in the snow. Nina scrambled off her back.

"Get up, Zelda! Get up!"

The mare groaned.

"Papa!" Nina screamed. "Help me!" Nina cradled Zelda's lovely head and sobbed.

Then Viktor was by her side, shielding her from the weather. "I'm sorry, Nina. I'm afraid this may be the end for your brave old mare." His voice was filled with sadness.

"No!" Nina shook her head. "No, no, no!"

Viktor was silent for a moment. It was snowing hard now. If they left Zelda, she would be buried in no time.

"You have to ride with me now, Nina. We must move on quickly or we will perish too. I have to get the stallions to safety."

Nina looked hard at her father. "We can't desert Zelda now," she pleaded. "She saved our lives."

Viktor put his arms around his daughter. "All right," he said. "We will try. Help me push her."

They rocked Zelda to and fro, but she was too exhausted to stand.

"Please, Papa. You have to get her up," Nina cried.

Viktor put his arms under the mare's hindquarters and pushed with all his strength.

"Come on, Zelda," Nina begged. "Come on . . ."

Z ELDA STRUGGLED onto shaky legs.

"You've done it, Papa," said Nina. "She's standing!
Will she be all right now?"

"I don't know," he replied. "It's up to Zelda.
We can't make her walk. She has to want to come
with us."

Viktor lifted Nina onto his horse, and they set off
again. Nina turned and called, "Zelda! Come on!"

Zelda stood still, and Nina's heart did too.
Then the old mare took a step. Then another . . .
and another . . .

In the evening they emerged from the trees to see
the last rays of the sun coloring the sky. Far below
in the darkening valley stood a cottage with light
shining from every window.

"Look," said Viktor. "We are nearly there. You
will see your grandparents soon."

But Nina was so exhausted, she could hardly
hear him.

As THEY CROSSED the dark valley, a dog began to bark. The cottage door opened.

"Is that you, Viktor?" a voice called out.

They rode toward the light, and Viktor passed Nina down into her grandmother's arms. She carried Nina into the warm cottage.

"This was your mother's bed," her grandmother said as she tucked Nina in. "My Anna slept here when she was a little girl."

Nina's sleepy eyes rested on an embroidered orange horse beside the bed. It's just like mine, she thought dreamily, then suddenly sat up in a panic.

"Where's Zelda?" she asked. "Did she follow us? I tried to keep calling her, but I was so tired. . . ."

"It's all right," said her grandmother, smoothing Nina's hair. "Zelda is here."

Nina pushed back the covers. "I need to see her!"

They hurried through the cold night to the warm barn. Inside, the horses stood like statues. Nina's grandfather carried pails of water to their stalls, and Viktor rubbed Zelda down while she ate steadily.

Viktor smiled at Nina. "We've saved them," he said. "The stallions are safe. We are all safe."

Nina gently rubbed Zelda's ears. "And Zelda saved us. She may be just an old cab horse, but she saved our lives."

For my goddaughter, Hilary

AUTHOR'S NOTE

Running with the Horses is a work of fiction. The story was inspired by the rescue of the Lipizzaner stallions from the Spanish Riding School in Vienna during the Second World War but is not intended to be an historical or accurate portrayal of that rescue or any related events or circumstances.

ACKNOWLEDGMENTS

Running with the Horses has been a long time in the making. I would like to thank Rita Hart, who has guided
and nurtured the book all the way, and Jane Godwin and Amy Thomas of Penguin Group (Australia) for their
excellent editing. I am grateful to all at Penguin who have contributed their time and thought to the project
over the years. Many thanks also to Elisa Webb for her sensitive design; Jade O'Connell for the digital
roughs; Joan Liley and Elke Beikufner for their photographs; Sandy Anderson and Bridget Fleming for
acting as models; Dr. Jaromir Oulehla and the Spanish Riding School in Vienna, who allowed me
to visit; and Johanna Reigler, who graciously spent time showing me the Winter Palace.

First published in the United States in 2011 by North-South Books Inc.,
an imprint of NordSüd Verlag AG, CH-8005 Zürich, Switzerland.
Distributed in the United States by North-South Books Inc., New York 10001.

Library of Congress Cataloging-in-Publication Data is available.
Printed in China by Leo Paper Products Ltd., Heshan, Guangdong, September 2010.
ISBN: 978-0-7358-4002-7 (trade edition)
1 3 5 7 9 • 10 8 6 4 2

www.northsouth.com